AF584302

IDAN BEN-BARAK and ZAHRA ZAINAL

How Do I Know If I'm Upside Down?

(And other things my body knows)

A Scholastic Press book from Scholastic Australia

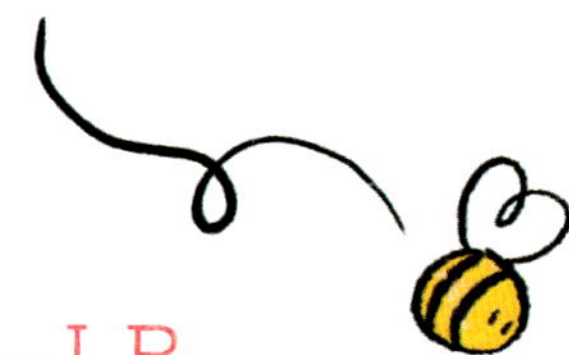

For Suzy and Alma – I.B.
For Papa and Mama – Z.Z.

Scholastic Press
An imprint of Scholastic Australia Pty Limited (ABN 11 000 614 577)
PO Box 579 Gosford NSW 2250
www.scholastic.com.au

Part of the Scholastic Group
Sydney • Auckland • New York • Toronto • London • Mexico City
New Delhi • Hong Kong • Buenos Aires • Puerto Rico

Published by Scholastic Australia in 2024.

A catalogue record for this book is available from the National Library of Australia

ISBN: 978-1-76112-137-1

Book design by Astred Hicks.
The illustrations in this book were created digitally.

Printed in China by RR Donnelley.
Scholastic Australia's policy, in association with RR Donnelley, is to use papers that are renewable and made efficiently from wood grown in responsibly managed sources, so as to minimise its environmental footprint.

10 9 8 7 6 5 4 3 2 1 24 25 26 27 28 / 2

This is me.

Light comes from
the SUN

or a FIRE

or a LIGHTBULB.

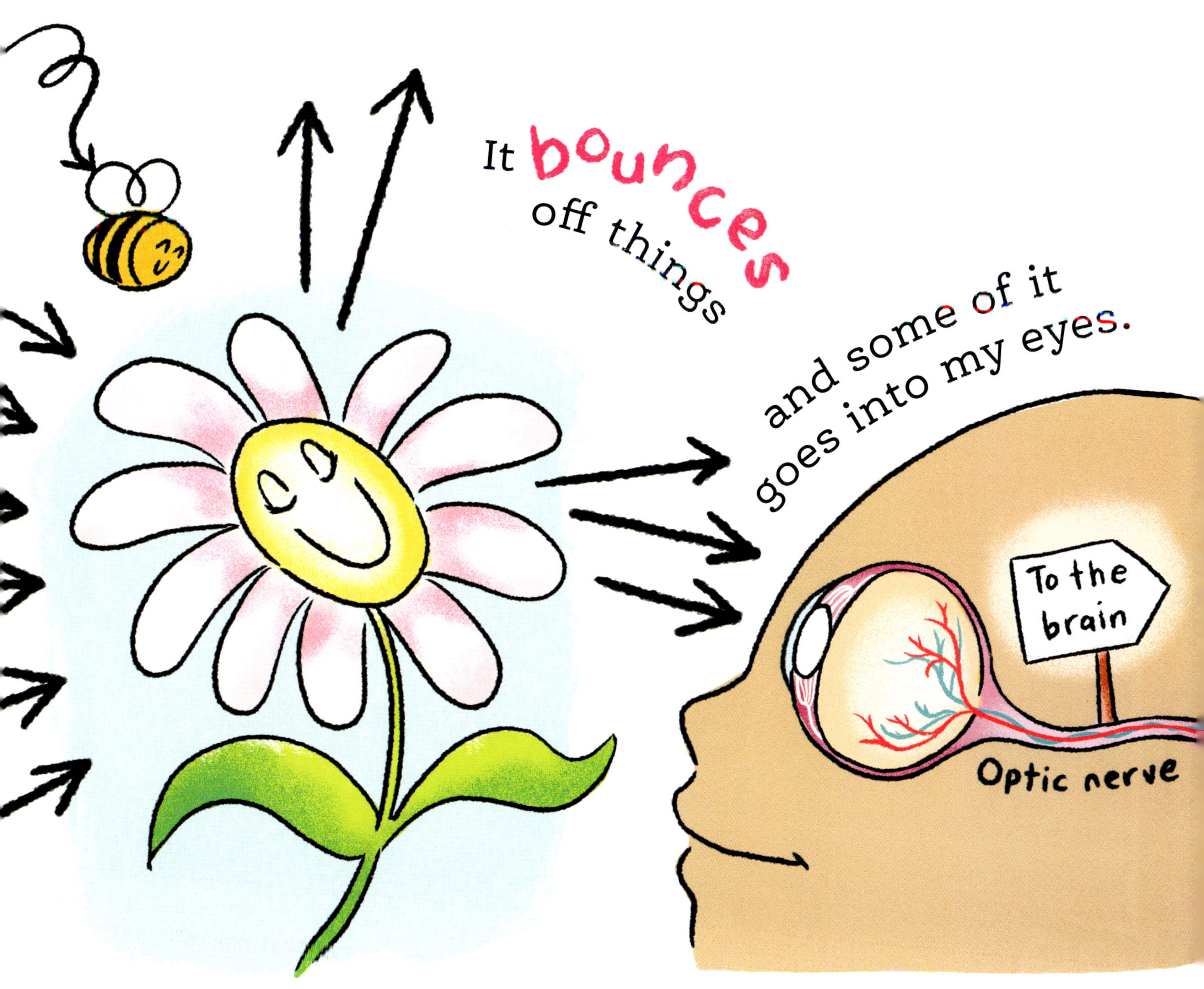

My eyes tell my brain what's going on.
That's how I **SEE**.

Air can move in

FAST WAVES.

When these **ENTER** my ear . . .

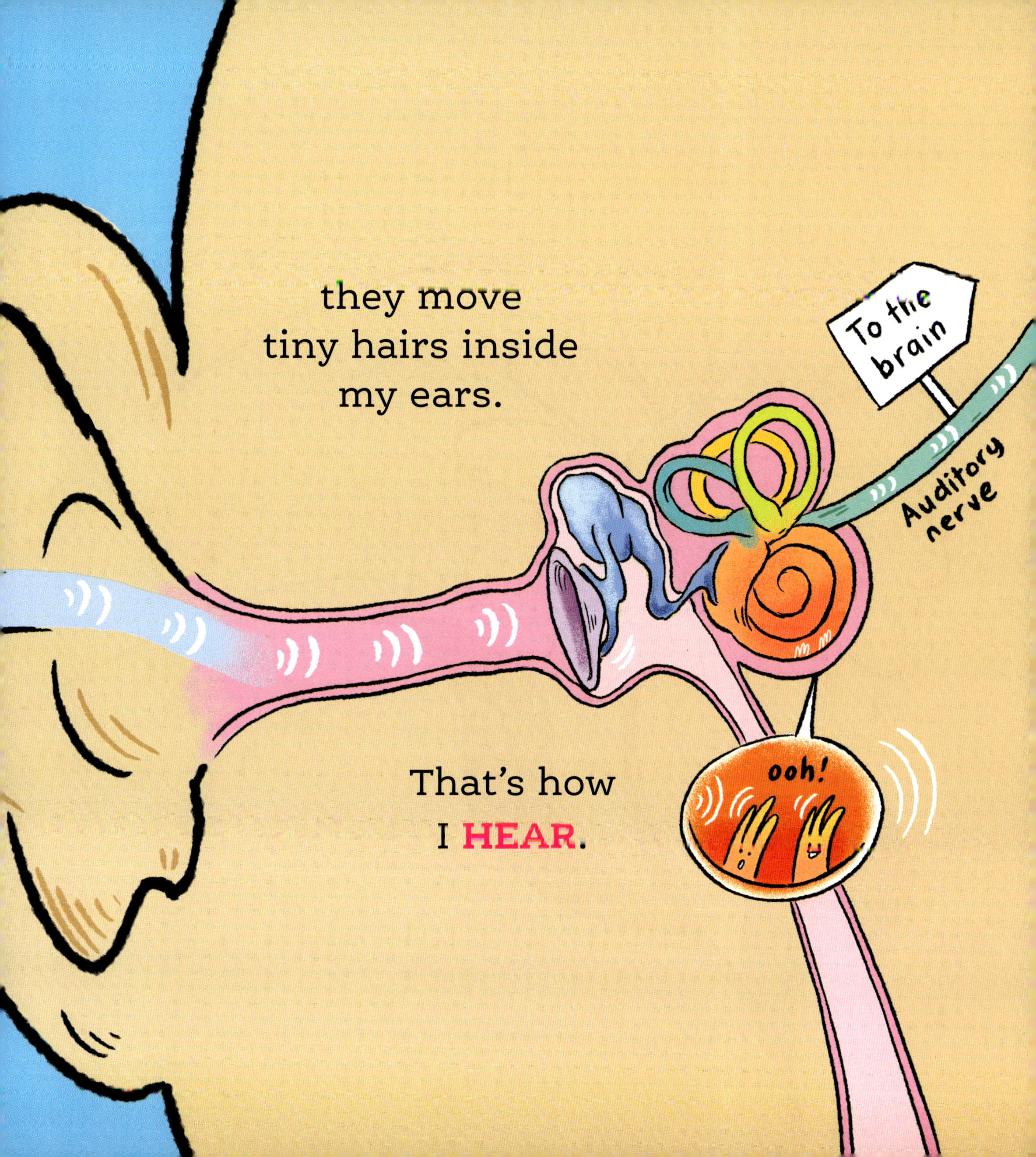

they move
tiny hairs inside
my ears.

That's how
I **HEAR**.

When tiny things called **MOLECULES** spray into the air . . .

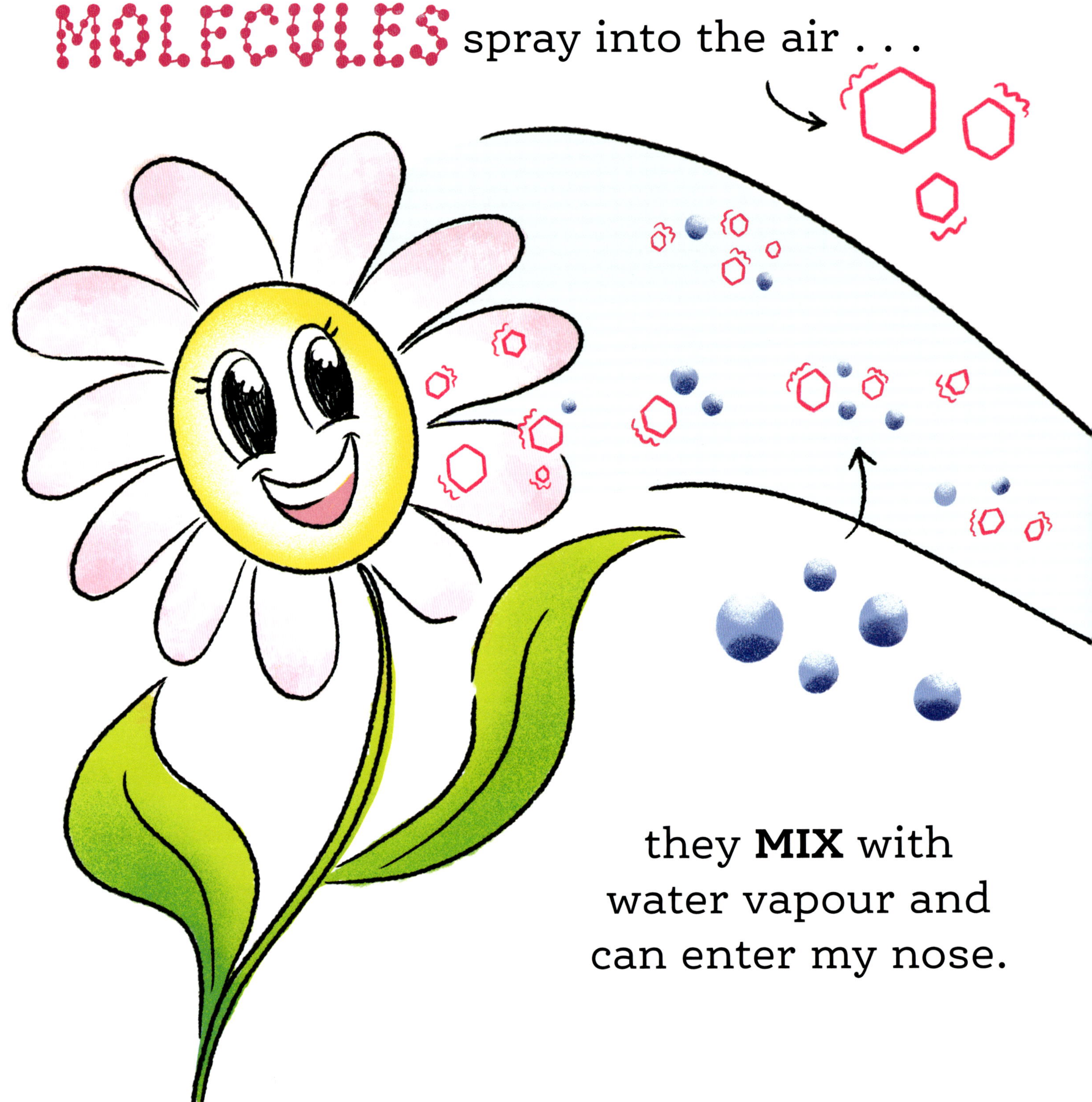

they **MIX** with water vapour and can enter my nose.

Nerves inside my nose can tell what those molecules are.

That's how I **SMELL** things.

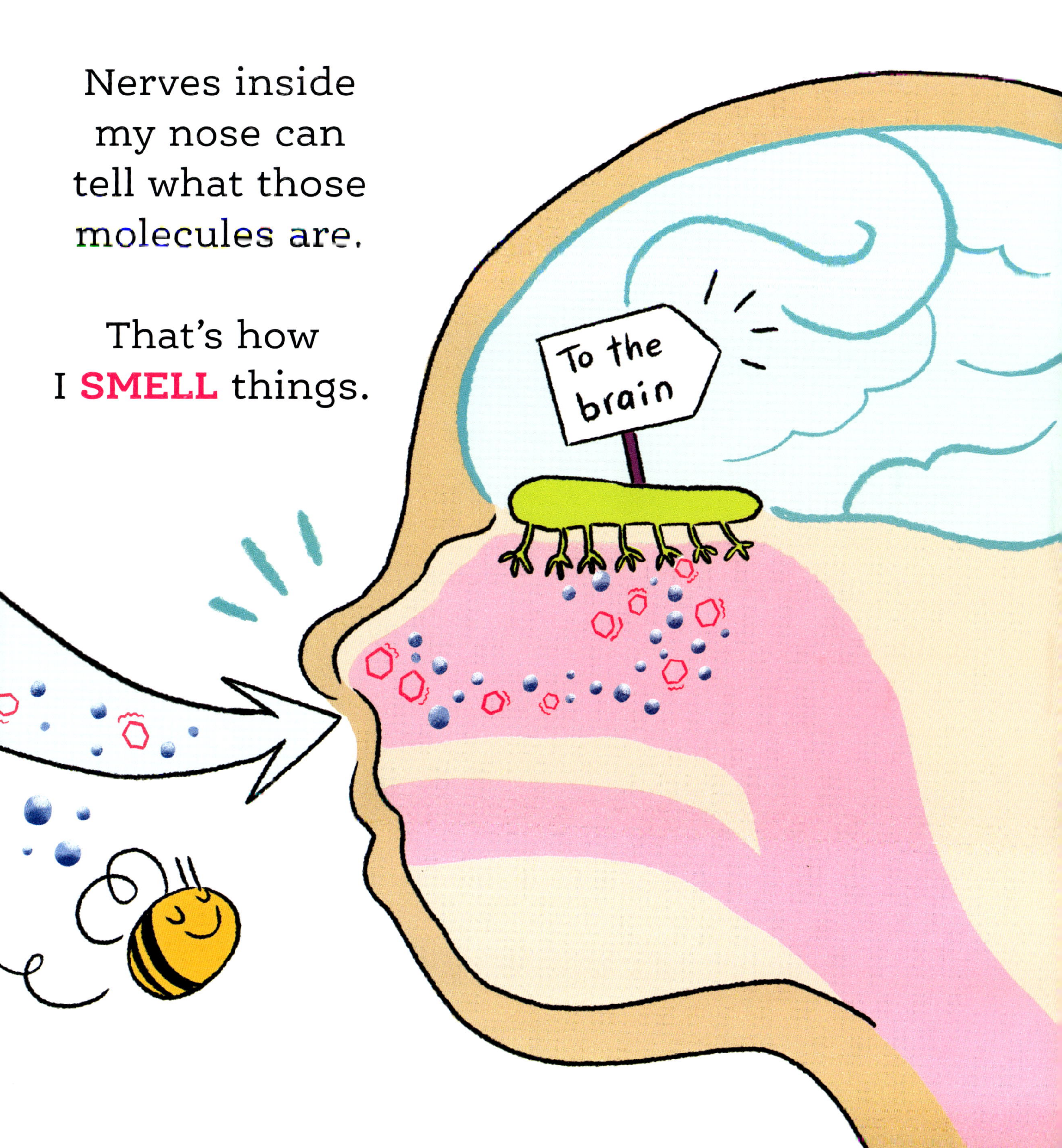

When molecules get in my mouth, my **TONGUE** can tell what some of them **ARE**.

That's how I **TASTE**.

When something **TOUCHES** my skin, **NERVES** in my skin can tell whether it is

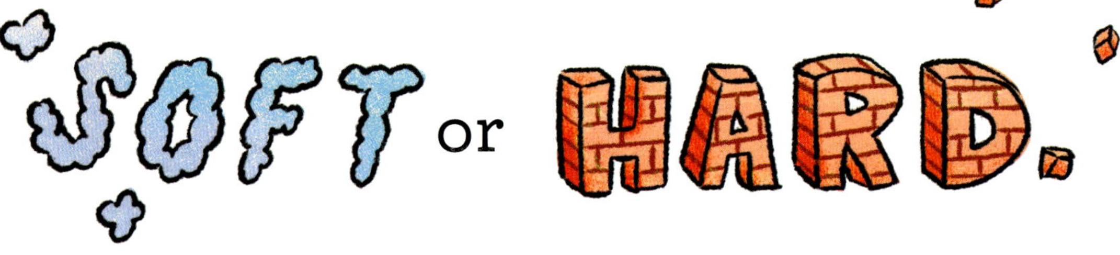

That's my sense of **TOUCH**.

Activate!

But that's not **ALL**
my body knows.

My body knows

My body knows if it is

or SIDEWAYS.

A little organ in my ear can tell, and it tells my brain.

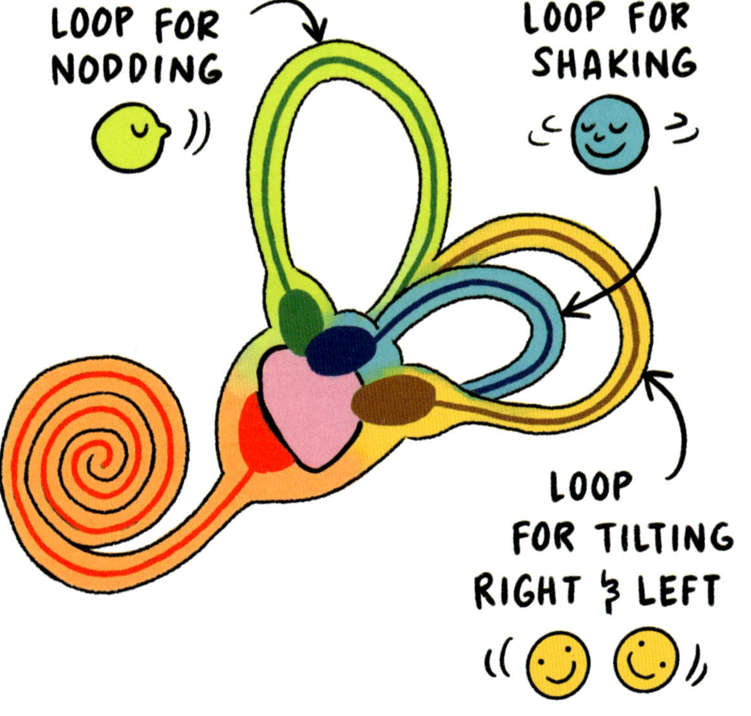

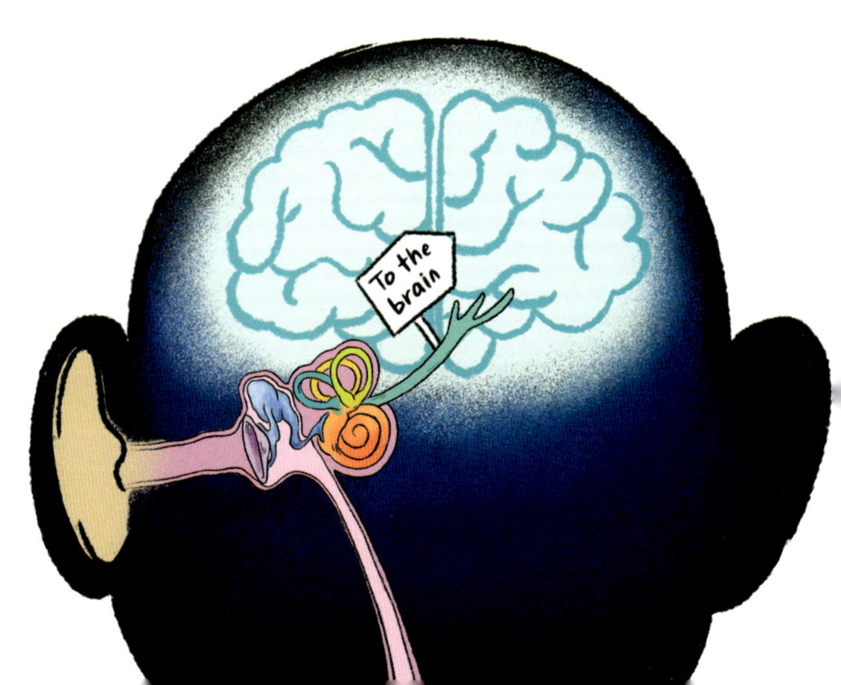

If I spin
around

TOO FAST

it can get **CONFUSED**

and I feel *dizzy*.

My body **KNOWS** if something is wrong.

It can feel

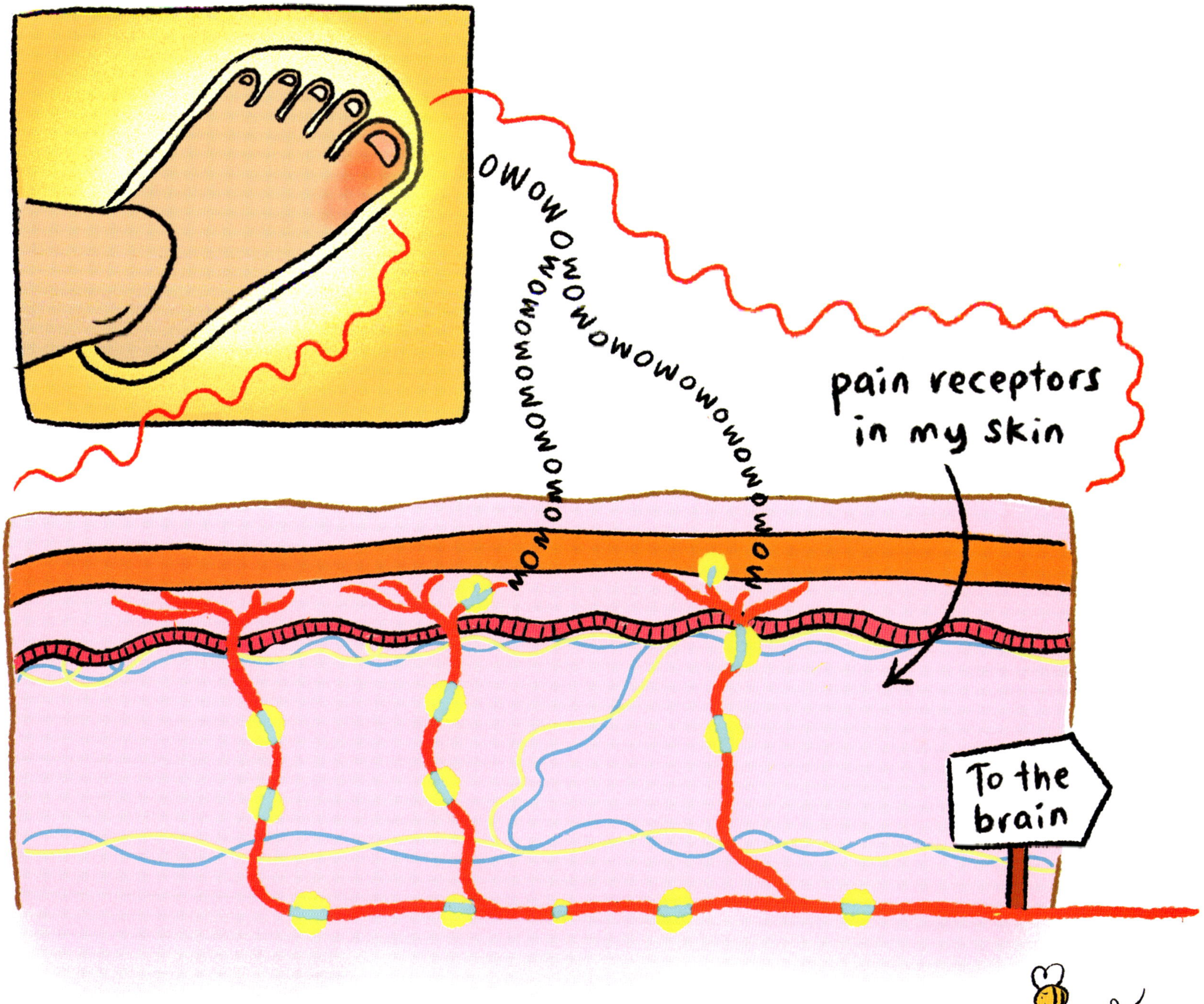

. . . and my brain knows not
to do that thing again.

My body knows **WHERE** my **ARMS** and **LEGS** are, even when I close my eyes and don't touch anything.

Nerves inside
my muscles can
tell if they're

or if I'm holding
something

My body knows if my
TUMMY is **FULL**.

It also knows when my **BLADDER** is **FULL**

(and I need to pee).

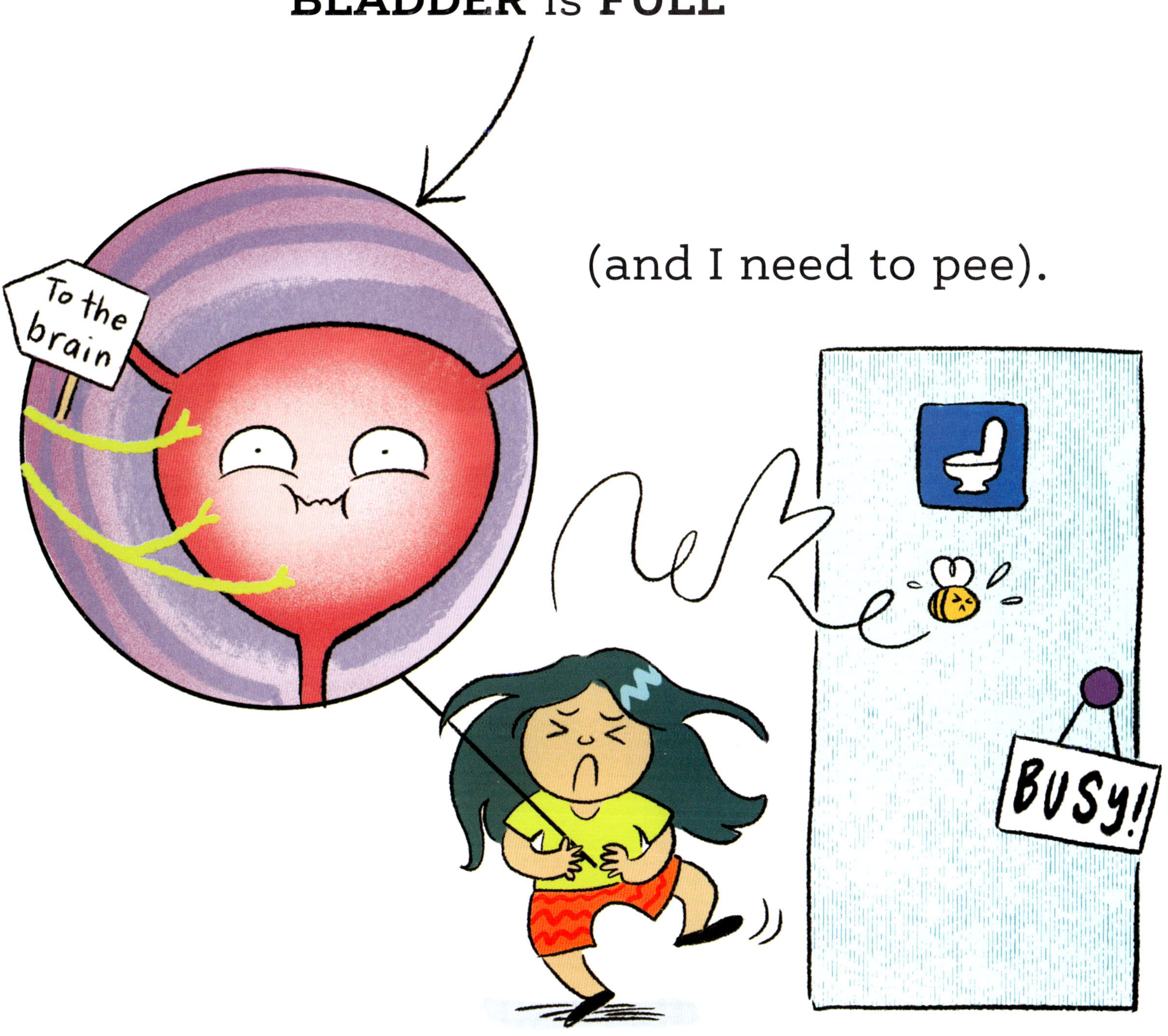

My body knows if it's

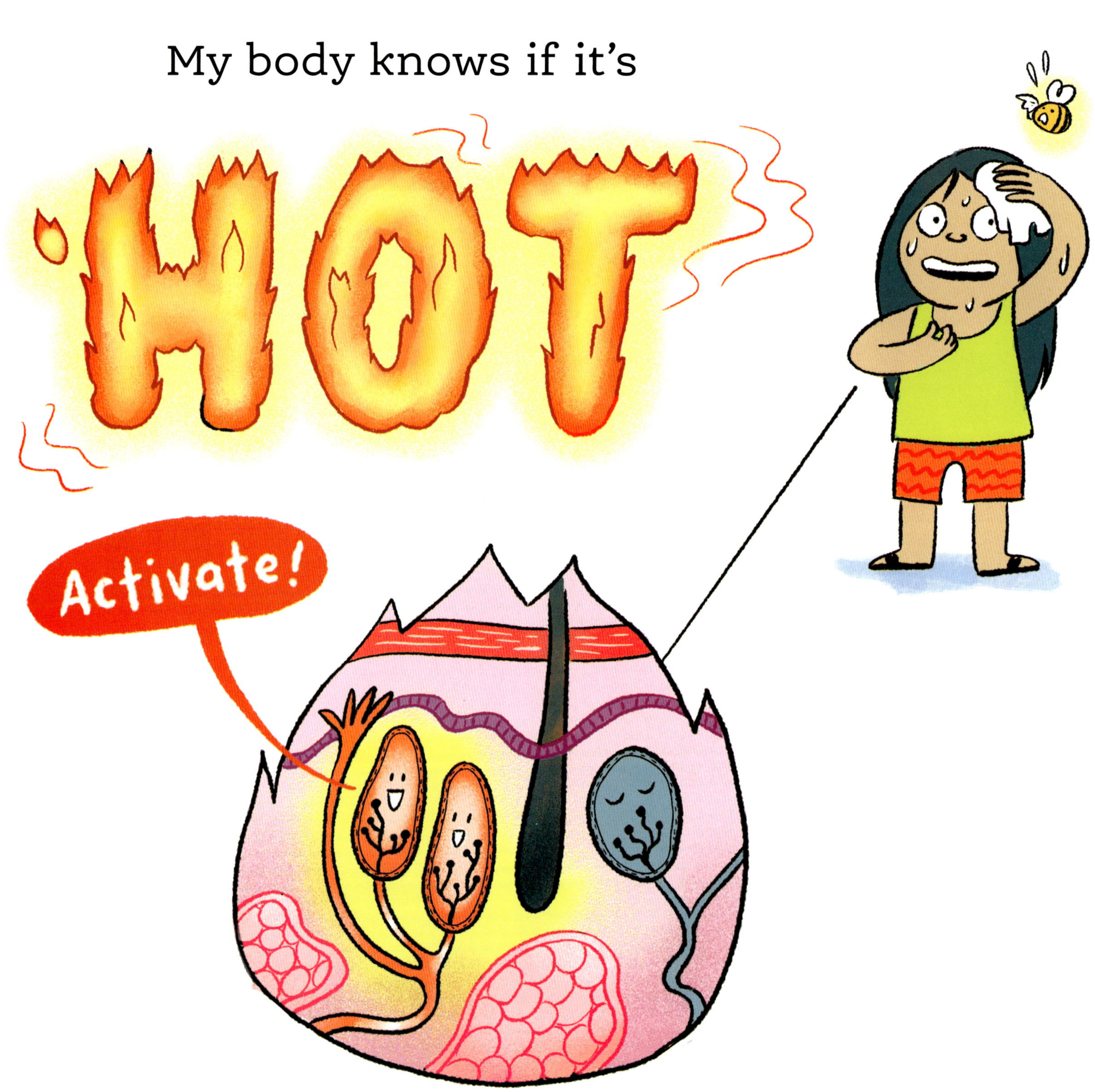

or

outside it.

My body knows **SO MANY THINGS!**

What Other Bodies Know

We can sing songs . . .

My body knows which direction it is, like a compass, so I don't get lost.

Mine too.

Homing pigeon

Bogong moth

Pit viper

I can sense heat from a distance.

My body knows when there are others like me around.

Drosophila fruit fly

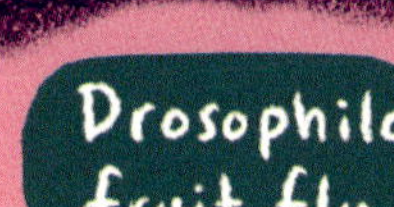

Cockroach

I can smell water.

Me too.

Hi!
Elephant
I can hear for many miles with my legs.
Hi!
. . . across an entire ocean.
Humpback whale
My body knows when electricity is in water.
Platypus
I'm just unbelievably awesome.
Mantis shrimp

My body can see

COLOURS that others can't.

My body can see things with **SOUND**, even in the dark.

Our
KNOW

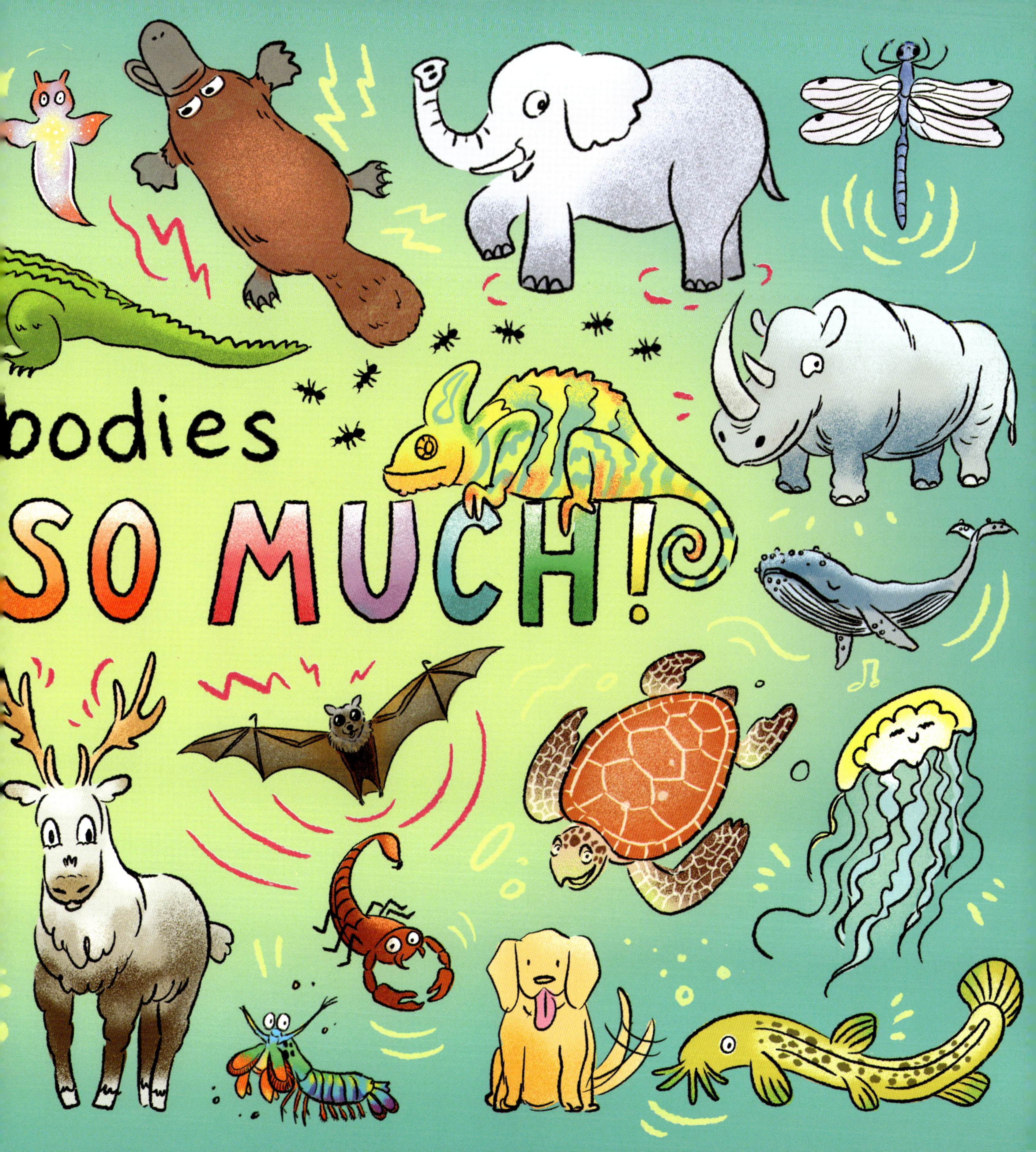

bodies
SO MUCH!

Hey, what about ME?!
I can sense magnetic fields!
And ultraviolet light!
And humidity!
And I can hear with my legs and talk with my sense of smell and by dancing, and the electricity of a flower can tell me whether other bees have visited it and . . .